BUNNIE THE BUNNY
WITH
BUGSY THE BUNNY

our lives and other bits

GARY PAUL STEPHENSON

Pharos Books

ISBN: 978-93-59837-78-9
eISBN: 978-93-59830-69-8

Copyright © 2024 by Gary Paul Stephenson

Publisher: Pharos Books (P) Ltd.
Plot No.-63, 1st Floor, Main Mother Dairy Road
Pandav Nagar, East Delhi-110092 (India)
Phone: +014049995474
WhatsApp: +91 9319228272
E-mail: sales@pharosbooks.in
Website: www.pharosbooks.in
Edition: 2024

Bunnie the Bunny with Bugsy the Bunny
Author: Gary Paul Stephenson

CONTENTS

Who am I?

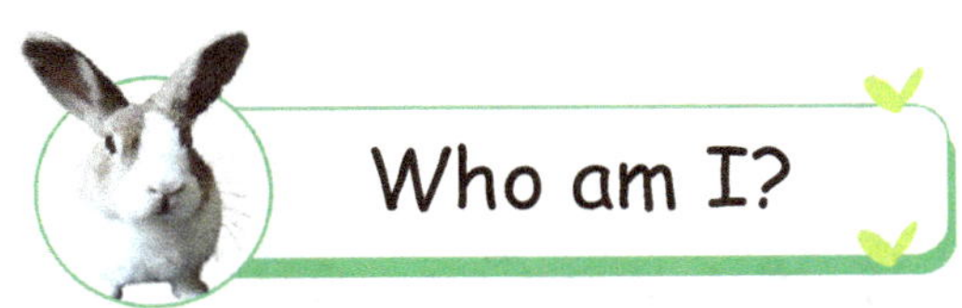

Hi, Bunnie here along with my brother, Bugsy. If you have met us before in our two previous books you will know that we are Dutch rabbits, with colourful apricot and white soft fur.

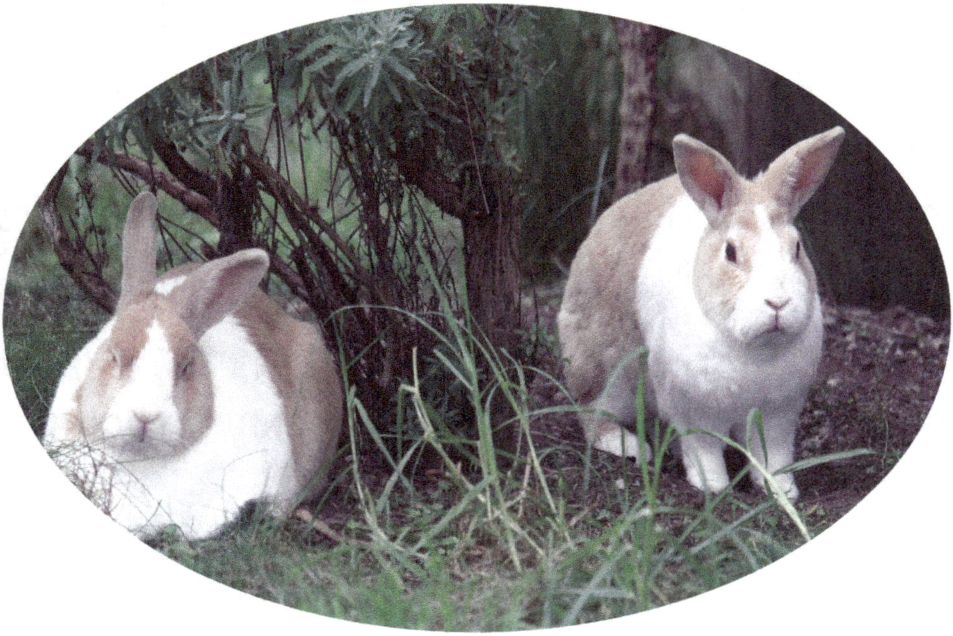

Bugsy and I are house bunnies and we have lived with Mum and Dad since we were six weeks old; we are now nine years old. In human years we would be sixty-nine! Wow! That is old. How old are you? Due to our age, we are on medications each day which Mum or Dad gives us in the morning and evening via syringes. We both enjoy taking our medicine and if Mum walks in our room and says 'medicine' we both go running over to her. Our favourite is the one that tastes like honey! Yum! Recently I had to have a strawberry flavored medicine that was horrible! Mum and Dad tried to hide the taste by mixing it with one of the other medicines, but I knew what they were up to and refused to take it! You cannot fool me! Us bunnies are very smart.

Bugsy and I get on very well as brother and sister. Bugsy is my physical support whereby if there is danger then he will attack whatever that danger may be. He fluffs his fur up and makes himself look bigger and more threatening, then he will go forward with his head lowered and stare down at the intruder. Bugsy is my great protector. Whereas Bugsy needs me for his emotional support whereby he comes to find me, sits beside me, lays

beside me, cuddles up to me and seeks me out
if he feels worried or lonely.

    Bugsy and I have unique, distinct, and
individual personalities, just like humans. Also
like humans, we love to be part of the family.
Keeping us inside allows us to be friendly and
express our personalities, whether that be
gentle and cuddly, or feisty and opinionated.
Cuddling and petting Bugsy and I is enjoyable
for both us and our Mum and Dad as is bonding
with us, getting to watch our amusing behaviour,
and getting comfort by our presence.

If Bugsy or I feel insulted or put out, then we will turn our backs on whomever has caused us to be upset! Sometimes, a simple stroke on the forehead or an apologetic treat can turn us round! Saying 'sorry' also!

Our Mum and Dad like to talk to us. When Bugsy and I are travelling in the car then Mum and Dad tell us where we are going, how long the journey will be and who we are going to see. In the house, when we are resting, Mum and Dad come and sit or lay down beside us and chat to us making sure that we are ok. Bugsy and I enjoy these chats and respond by twitching our mouths as if in answer to them. This is our way of talking and means we are happy and content. We can hold quite an interesting conversation in bunny language!

We show our Mum and Dad how happy we are by licking their nose if they put their face close to ours. If they put their head close, then we will groom them by pulling at their hair. This is our way of saying that they are part of our family, and we are part of theirs.

Platforms or steps that require us to climb or hop up and down are great fun and help Bugsy and I to use our muscles and strengthens our bones.

Us rabbits need space - think garden shed, rather than a cramped hutch. Our home needs to be tall enough for us to be able to stand up fully without our ears touching the roof and to lie fully outstretched in any direction, to take hops and to run, jump, explore, forage, and do all the things that come naturally to us bunnies.

Bugsy and I are curious and intelligent animals and need toys to play with. Our favorite toys are cardboard tubes as they are light enough for us to pick up with our mouths and toss in the air. Sometimes Mum and Dad fill these tubes with hay so that we pull out long strands to eat. Just like eating spaghetti!

While you may think Bugsy and I as just a pet, we are an 'exotic' pet. This means if we need a visit to a veterinarian, we must go to a vet that specialises in treating us – rather than a vet that specialises in treating just dogs or cats. I am a female rabbit or 'doe,' and Bugsy is a male rabbit or 'buck.' Young rabbits are known as kits. When I was a kit the vet spayed me which means that I cannot be a mum to any kits of my own but also helps lower the chance of me getting a horrible disease called cancer. The vet also neutered Bugsy which means he cannot be a dad to any kits but also helps reduce any bad temper behaviour – like biting. Neutering or spaying can also extend our lifespan by anything from about eight to twelve years! Bugsy and I have also been micro-chipped. This means that our vet has inserted a tiny computer chip just under the skin in our neck that identifies us. If Bugsy or I were to ever get lost or stolen, then if whoever found us took us to a vet, they would be able to scan this chip using a special machine and then we would get back home with our Mum and Dad. Happy days!

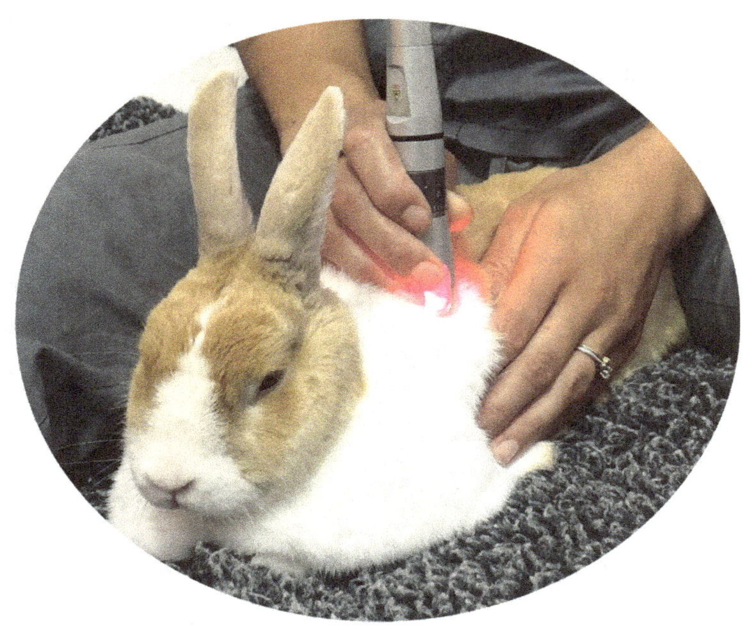

Whilst I am talking about the vets, then I just want to mention how important it is for

Bugsy and me to have the Filavie vaccination each year. This vaccine protects Bugsy and I from a very nasty disease. Our vet injects the vaccine into the scruff of our neck. This does not hurt at all. When Bugsy and I were ten weeks old we had our first vaccination which took twenty-one days to take full effect. As the virus can spread quickly through insects such as flies or contact with infected rabbits, then it is important for us to continue to have this annual booster shot.

Dad helps to control the spread of viruses by making sure that flies do not land on us by spraying Bugsy and I every three months with a special spray. Flies can cause 'flystrike', which if left untreated can be deadly. When we are in the garden Mum or Dad are always outside with us. Our back garden has been cat proofed to prevent access by stray cats. When Dad cuts the grass for us then he cuts with scissors as lawn mower cut grass can make us sick. Also, when the new season grass has grown in Spring, then trimming the top couple of inches or centimetres off before we can feed on the grass will ensure that the grass is not too rich for our tummies!

If we are not feeling very well, then we will sit quietly away from everybody and not eat or drink. If anybody comes to check up on us then we will move away and keep changing our sitting position as we are feeling uncomfortable. This is a cry for help and will require a visit to the vet for a checkup. Do you have tummy ache? Not nice, is it? As we have an incredibly special digestive system, we must continue to eat and drink as we can get seriously ill very quickly.

At night to settle down ready for sleep I enjoy having my cheek rubbed. I close my eyes and settle down on our blanket with my legs tucked under my body or I will flop on my side and stretch out.

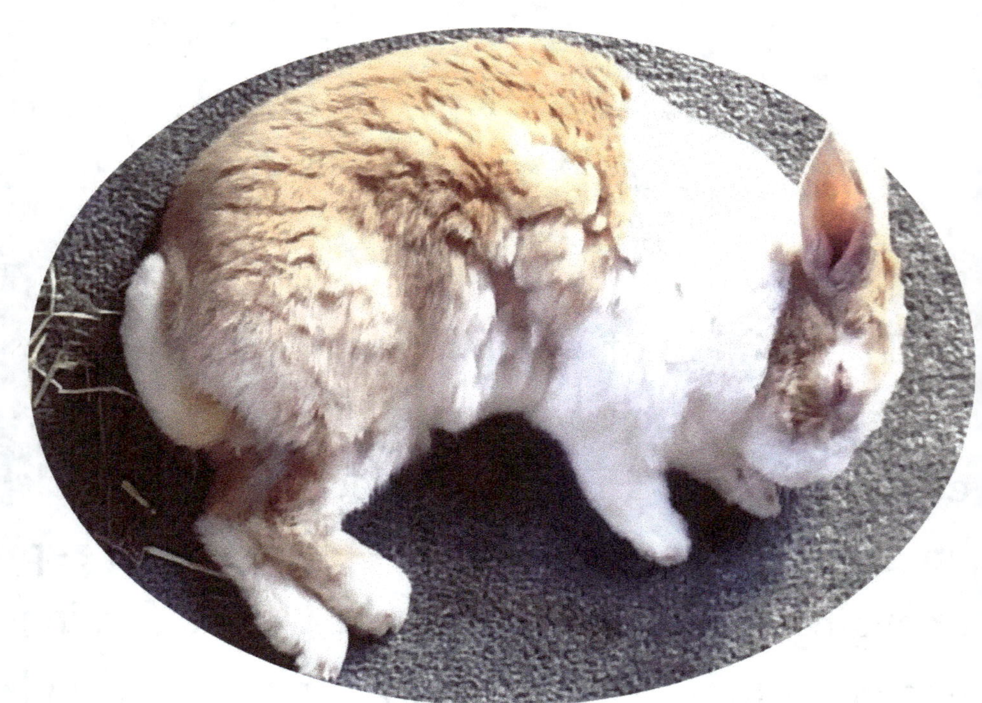

Although rabbits are not supposed to enjoy having their tummy rubbed, Bugsy does! He is an such an unusual rabbit! When we are happy then our mouths twitch and we sometimes chatter our teeth together. Does that put your teeth on edge? Do you know that our teeth do not stop growing? Unlike humans, Bugsy and my teeth continue to grow throughout our lifetime – in fact, they can grow between three to five inches (7.5 – 12cm) a year! That is why Bugsy and I need hay or wooden toys to chew so that we can keep our teeth ground down all the time. In the wild, our teeth would become ground down due to our diet of tough plant food. Our Mum and Dad help manage our teeth length by providing hay for us to nibble on twenty-four hours a day. Our top and bottom front teeth - called incisors - are even in length. Our vet checks that we have no cracks in our teeth and that our teeth do not move. Using a special instrument, the vet also checks our rear teeth which are impossible to see with the naked eye. I am not very fond of

that happening! Do you go to the dentist? No
the pleasantest of experiences, is it?

When we chew our food then we can chew
as much as 120 times per minute, and we have
over 17000 taste buds in our mouths. That
is why we always hunt out the best tasting
food whether it be grass, hay, greens, pellets
herbs, or fruit leaves.

Our ears serve two main purposes. The first and most obvious is hearing. Us rabbits can rotate our ears 270 degrees, which allows us to detect any threats that might be approaching close to us or as far as two miles away. Our oversized ears also have the added benefit of cooling us down on a sweltering day as the surface area means body heat can escape.

It is hard to sneak up on us rabbits as our vision covers close to a full 360 degrees so we can see all around us at once! This allows us to see what is coming in the distance in front of us, from behind us, from above us, and from either left or right sides without turning our heads. This is known as long-sighted vision. We have a small blind spot directly in front of our nose which makes us short-sighted for nearer objects. This is why sometimes we will not be able to sniff out immediately that special treat put in front of our noses! Our vision is monocular – meaning we only use one eye when looking to either side or behind us, but our vision is binocular when looking straight ahead – meaning we use both eyes. We recognise patterns and objects best if they are in front of us. We see colour but are red-green colour blind. This means we can easily confuse any colours which have red or green as part of the whole colour. We could therefore confuse blue with purple because we cannot see the red element in the colour purple. Our vision is adapted to see predators quickly from any angle, especially if we are out feeding at dawn or dusk when the light is dim. This is why we can see better in poor light that humans can.

Bugsy and I both must do exercises twice per day – morning and evening. I must do four paw stretches as I have a sore left front paw and am putting too much weight on my good right paw. Each time I put my paw on the ground it hurt me. Along with the exercises I also have two minutes of infrared. This is a machine that Mum holds under my sore paw and a red-light glow from led bulbs helps to heal the paw. Now my paw is getting better. I do not like Dad picking me up, but once Dad has settled me in his arms then I am happy. Bugsy has more exercises to do than me, but he is very patient and lets Mum and Dad get on with it. Mum holds him and talks to him whilst Dad helps Bugsy with the exercises. All these exercises make Bugsy and I tired, so after we have had a treat for being good, we tend to have a rest.

Grooming

Bugsy and I are clean animals, and we like our areas that we lie and play in to be clean too. Dad tidies our room every day. Mum cleans our food and water bowls every day. Mum also empties and cleans our litter trays daily and changes our bedding on a regular basis.

Bugsy and I keep ourselves clean by licking ourselves or each other. This is known as 'grooming.' We do not need baths as we clean ourselves thoroughly throughout the day. Do you have a bath, or do you prefer a shower? Grooming is not only a solo activity; Bugsy and I use grooming to enhance our bond with each other and to establish the order of dominance. I like to think that I am the dominant one! I am in charge! I will frequently shove my head underneath Bugsy's chin and demand grooming! However, as we are siblings and have such a good relationship, he will also shove his head underneath my chin and demand grooming! Like sister, like brother!

Bugsy and I enjoy grooming each other - called 'mutual grooming.' This means that each of us can get to areas of each other's bodies that are difficult for us to get to. This is important and is part of our bonding process. As part of our grooming, Bugsy and I lick our fur to clean it, remove any dirt, and loose hair. As well as providing care for us and ensuring our good health, regular grooming is the best way for Dad and Mum to spend time and bond with us.

Part of Bugsy and my grooming routine means checking and cleaning our eyes and ears.

Small particles can easily get into these areas and cause discomfort or infection. Bugsy and I will sit up on our rear hind legs and lift our front paws to our head to wipe away anything that is irritating our eyes or ears. Bugsy has eye and ear drops every day as he can suffer from dry eye where his eyes do not get enough moisture and wax build up in his ears. If Bugsy has trouble with his ears, then he will shake his head from side to side and as he has trouble scratching his ears, ear drops help him. Our eyes, nose and ears should always be clean, with no matted fur or any funny smell. Our eyes should be bright. If we sneeze, then we should not sneeze more than once or twice in a row.

We can shed our fur up to four times per year. As we are short haired bunnies then our heaviest shedding of fur is usually at the end of winter when we get rid of our thicker fur and again at the end of summer when we shed our lighter fur. Our skin is quite fragile, so Dad uses a brush specially designed for rabbits and brushes gently first in the direction of our fur and then against. Dad brushes Bugsy and I daily so that when we groom ourselves or each other we do not swallow too much fur as this can give us fur balls and cause us to feel ill as the fur blocks our digestive system. This can mean a visit to the vet for special medicine to get our gut working normally again.

Mum and Dad check if our chin or insides of our front legs are wet, as this can indicate 'drooling' which may mean we have teeth problems. If the soles of our front or back paws have a small raised red area, then this can indicate 'sore hocks' and we will need special ointment applied to ease our pain. I tend to suffer with sore rear hocks and Mum applies this sticky ointment which if I get the chance I will lick! Naughty but nice! To get round this, Mum uses my fur that is on the brush and uses the sticky ointment to stick the fur to the sore area as protection.

If you look at us from above, we should look slightly pear shaped! If we are more rounded – look like an apple with a head - then we are getting too fat and need to go on a diet!

Bugsy and I keep each other company, groom each other and have fun together. In the wild, Bugsy and I would be living in a group with other rabbits. Bugsy and I have bonded, and will be partners for life, and we spend our time snuggling and grooming each other.

When we dream, our head moves up and down, our paws and mouth twitch but we do not make any sounds. Do you dream?

Foraging

Bugsy and I are so lucky as though we are indoor rabbits, we also benefit from being able to get outdoors when the weather is right as well. We enjoy the grass, sunshine and fresh air that going outside gives us but also enjoy the indoor lifestyle. Best of both worlds! Us bunnies can be excellent escape artists and can tunnel, gnaw, or wriggle our way through all manner of cracks and crevices so we must have a secure area with things for us to do so we do not get bored and try to tunnel out! To make sure that we are safe Mum or Dad is always in the garden with us so they can watch over us just in case.

Bugsy and I enjoy grazing, and we will happily graze all day long especially if we are outside eating grass. Our garden is set up with four types of grass so that we can choose which one we want to graze on as we wander around the garden. When we can get into the garden to eat the fresh grass then we also nibble the lavender and rosemary bushes. Tasty treats! Both the flowers and the leaves are edible. Foraging for 'common or garden' weeds such as clover, daisies, and dandelions growing amongst the grass are great for stopping us from getting bored. We also have a blackberry bush and lemon trees in our garden, but we must not eat the fruit – just the leaves. Occasionally, Dad will give us a lemon twig to chew which is good for our teeth. Apple twigs are also tasty to chew – we strip the bark off the stick. In the springtime Bugsy and I also like to chew on willow twigs. All these twigs are delicious!

In the summer months our Mum and Dad sometimes set up a big tub of sand outside for Bugsy and me to dig in or lie in depending on how energetic we feel! When Bugsy and I cannot play outside – especially during the winter months when it is too cold or too wet – our Mum and Dad put our pellets in a special toy where Bugsy and I must open or push / pull off lids to find our pellets. Playful fun! Bugsy and I both love these feeding toys! Mum or Dad will mix up fennel fern, parsley leaf, rocket, thyme, mint, lavender, and rosemary leaves on a plate of grass when we cannot get outside as it is too wet or cold. The grass strands are nice and long and sometimes we take such a big bite it looks as though we have a green beard!

Whether we are inside or outside it is important that the temperature is not too hot, nor too cold, not too dry, nor too humid, well-aired but not draughty. Sixteen to twenty degrees is ideal. Below sixteen degrees is getting a bit too cold, and we need a snuggle pad. Higher than twenty degrees is getting too hot, and we can suffer from heatstroke. Any area that is too damp or draughty, or is not well-aired, is much more likely to cause us to become ill. In the winter Bugsy and I have self-reflecting heat fleeces and blankets to lie on along with a heat pad to keep us warm. In the summer we have cool pads and sheets to lie on to keep us cool. Bugsy and I have heavy water bowls that we cannot knock over which help keep the water chilled, and adding ice cubes to the water in the summer helps to keep the water chilled longer.

Bugsy and my daily diet are fresh hay or grass, the best quality pellets, and fresh water. Anything other than these are a treat' which Dad gives for good behaviour occasionally to ensure we are getting all the nutrition we need to stay healthy.

In the morning whilst Mum and Dad have a cup of tea, as part of our varied diet Bugsy and I have rabbit pellets for breakfast. I normally finish my pellets first, so I let Mum stroke me whilst Bugsy finishes his. Then when Bugsy has finished, he comes to lay beside me so that Mum can stroke both of us. We enjoy the cuddle after being on our own in our own room overnight. We miss Mum and Dad!

Bugsy or I will toss strands of hay away
if we think that it is not suitable for us to
eat! We like the freshest hay possible and
like to have fresh hay every day. We will
each eat an amount equal to the size of our
body in hay a day. If it smells nice then that
means it is fresh. If it is crisp, we will enjoy
sniffing out the tastiest pieces. Bugsy and I
are very particular about what we eat. Once
the hay goes feathery then all it is good for
is bedding as we will not eat it.

Fresh clean hay, or even better, fresh grass makes up much of our diet and keeps us healthy and happy plus stops us from getting bored. Hay or grass is important for us rabbits as it provides us with fibre and calories. It also keeps our gut moving, keeps our teeth healthy and controls caecal poops. Us rabbits produce two types of poops – normal hard, round poops and caecal poops. These caecal poops are small grape-like poops which provide essential amino acids and are a crucial energy source - yep, we eat our own poop! You will not usually see these small grape-like poops as we try to eat them immediately. Mum and Dad are gardeners and are into composting, so all our normal poops along with our old hay goes into the compost bin. When all the compost has broken down into what looks like soil, then Dad and Mum spread it all over the vegetable garden. This helps the plants grow big and strong. We bunnies have our uses!

High fibre pellets make up part of our diet. Pellets are a source of calories, proteins, vitamins, minerals, and essential fatty acids. Our Mum and Dad measure out our pellets as unlimited pellets are not good for us.

Green veggies make up a small part of our diet as they provide vitamins, minerals, and water. Green leafy plants are best – the darker the green colour the better. However, iceberg lettuce is a no! On our Birthday we get a special cake.

Bugsy and I like to have free access to fresh, clean water in a water bowl rather than a sipper bottle as the bowl is much easier for us to drink from.

Treats only make up a small amount of our diet. Too many treats can put us off healthy food, so Dad uses them as a special reward for good behaviour. Just like too many sweets for humans! A high sugar diet can also grow more harmful bacteria which can lead to painful gas or GI Stasis. Hence why carrots are not good for us – too high in sugar which can cause tooth decay! Feed us only the green tops – they are delicious! Are you familiar with the cartoon character Bugs Bunny? He was always eating a carrot – but we cannot survive on this root vegetable alone. In fact, in the wild rabbits rarely eat root vegetables at all, preferring to munch on grasses and green leafy plants. Of course, the occasional small carrot is ok. Banana and watermelon are our two favourite fruits – just a small slice is all we need! We lick our lips until our mouths are clean to get as much of the flavour as possible. Wonderful! Do you have a favourite fruit?

Body Language

We have ways of showing when we are happy or excited: 'binkying' is when we jump in the air with all our paws off the ground and twist in mid-air then land back on the ground. Often we will binky while zooming at speed across the garden or in the house. At first this may look worrying, but it means our Mum and Dad are doing an excellent job and we are happy playful, and content! As a happy and 'hoppy' young rabbit, we will dart around, jump in the air, and even twist in a dance! Binkying means: 'Life is good!' How do you show when you are happy? As we get older, we tend to binky less.

Us rabbits are mostly silent creatures so the main way that we express ourselves is through body language. If we are happy and content when lying down, we might have our back legs stretched out behind us, or our back legs stuck out sideways, or we might have our legs tucked in under our body – just like a cat. If we are annoyed, unhappy, or upset then to show our annoyance we will thump our back feet and move away. Each time we move we will thump!

Like all rabbits, Bugsy and I have scent glands on our chins which we use to mark territories, objects and even people! Humans cannot detect the scent, but other rabbits can, and these scent marks mean: 'This is mine!'

If Bugsy or I nose-nudge our Mum or Dad, then this can mean one of three things: 'Pet me now,' 'Pay me attention' or 'Move out of my way.'

If Bugsy or I gently grind our teeth - which may sound to you like a cat purring – then this means that we are content. But if it sounds like loud grinding then that is a sign that we are uncomfortable and means that we are saying 'I'm in pain' and need to see a vet as soon as possible.

As Bugsy and I have ears that are straight up then these acts like radar, both ears forward mean: 'Something has caught my attention', one ear forward and one back means: 'I've noticed something, but it doesn't require my full attention', both ears back mean: 'It's all good and I can give my radar a rest'.

If Bugsy or I lick our Mum or Dad, then that means: 'I like you' and you are a wonderful bunny owner!

Bugsy and I will sometimes circle around our owners' feet - especially when they are about to give us a special treat like banana. This means we are eager to get their attention. If we follow them around then that means: 'I'm here, take notice of me!'

If Bugsy or I jump on the back of each other this means: 'I'm the dominant one and don't you forget it!'

If Bugsy and I flop on our side and lay still this means: 'I'm so relaxed.'

If Bugsy or I drop our head and hold our ears very flat against our head with our belly down this means: 'I'm scared.'

Bugsy or I will sometimes thump our rear feet and that means: 'I am nervous' or 'Please stop, I'm annoyed at you!'

Lunging is where Bugsy or I make a sudden movement towards somebody or animal that is annoying us with our head and tail up and ears back means: 'I don't like that, back off.'

If Bugsy or I pinch or nip then this means:' I want your attention,' 'move out of the way' or 'I'm giving you a warning.'

Occasionally, Bugsy or I will leave scattered droppings out of our litter box and that means that that area belongs to us. It is a way of us marking our territory against any intruders.

If Bugsy or I were to ever wag our tail, then this is a sign of defiance and is a form of back chatting to Dad or Mum. For instance, if Dad or Mum wanted us to come indoors, then we are probably saying:' I don't want to go in yet!'

If we do not like the way Dad or Mum have arranged items in our area, then we will push or toss objects around meaning: 'Keep your hands off my stuff!'

Bugsy and I and all our bunny friends tend to make three distinct types of sound – honking, thumping our big rear feet, or clicking our teeth. One of the most common sounds you may hear is a 'honking' – an attention seeking behaviour. It can also be a sign of agitation or a warning to other rabbits, people, or animals.

Bugsy will honk when threatened or to show he
is not happy with a situation. When happy, we
may 'purr' by clicking our teeth together. Does
that put your teeth on edge? It is a different
sound to teeth grinding or chattering however
as this can be a sign of pain or sickness. When
unhappy or nervous, we may 'thump' by taking
a back foot and thumping it on the ground. In
the wild this behaviour alerts other rabbits
that there is a danger nearby.

As Bugsy and I are 'prey' animals this means that we can fear anything - a new sound or something falling or dopped can startle us so much that we will run off scared. It is essential we feel safe in our home so we cannot harm ourselves on any sharp edges or get stuck in a small space. As we roam around indoors, and we are very curious creatures, Dad has made sure all the electrical cords have a special covering over them so that we cannot nibble them thinking they are roots! Bugsy and I do not want to get an electrical shock! Plus, the corners of indoor walls have a small plastic covering over them so that Bugsy and I do not nibble the wallpaper and pull it off the walls!

We have places where we can hide if a 'predator' appears, or a noise startles us. These are safe hidey-holes known as 'hop-in-hideouts' or 'hideaway boxes' which are big enough for us to stretch out comfortably and relax. Bugsy and I love our cardboard hideaway boxes which always have two entrance or exit holes. As we do not like getting trapped, giving us two exit holes means that we can always escape. We also enjoy running or hiding in 'cat tunnels'. As we are a house rabbit, we have a hiding place in every room that we have access to. When we are outdoors then we have other places for us to run to when frightened. Especially when a helicopter goes low, right over our house! Scary!

Rabbit Facts

There are different breeds of rabbits which have either lop-ears or upright ears. Bugsy and I are upright-eared bunnies, which means our ears are straight up. Lop eared are when the ears bend over and down. With our long ears we can move each ear independently and this means that we can hear in two directions at once! Clever hey? When we walk around on the floor we hop as our rear legs are much longer than our front legs. We are very curious animals and like to know what is going on and investigate new things. You will notice when you look at us that we breathe quite fast – normally 30 – 60 breaths per minute. Anything faster than this means that we could be stressed, hot or excited. Human breath rates are between 12 -20 breaths per minute.

Our cousins, the wild rabbits, travel huge distances every day. So do we! We like to have space, with secure areas to exercise and run around. In the wild, rabbits wear down their nails as they go about their day, hopping around, digging, foraging for food, and running away from predators. Our vet keeps an eye on our nail length and clips them when they have grown past the fur at the end of our feet. It is just like having your nails cut but not too short as that will hurt us and cause bleeding. Ouch!

Did you know that over the last few years, the number of pet rabbits in New Zealand has increased rapidly? With just over a 30% increase in the last ten years or so, over 120,000 of us furry friends are pets! Best of all, wherever NZ families have been able to house at least two rabbits this means that we have company of our own kind as we would in the wild. The average lifespan of us pet rabbits that are house bunnies is nine to twelve years. Whereas the average lifespan of a rabbit kept in a backyard hutch is less than half the lifespan of an average indoor rabbit! So, for better quality of life for us bunnies please keep us with you in the house wherever possible. We are easy to litter train and will use litter trays - just like a cat or small dog – just make sure you have at least one in each room wherever your rabbit spends his or her time!

Did you know that we are now the fourth most popular pet in New Zealand, after dogs, cats, and fish! The main reason people get rabbits is that they believe that rabbits will be fun for their children. However, we are not the easiest pets to look after and need an adult to keep an eye on what is happening whilst children are with their bunnies.

Did you know that pet rabbits are related to the wild European rabbit whose scientific name is 'Oryctolagus cuniculus,' which mean 'hare-like digger of underground passages.' Quite appropriate do you think!

Did you know that wild rabbits when foraging for food can cover up to five miles per day. So, us pet bunnies need room to move around, with opportunity to exercise.

Bugsy and I hope that you have enjoyed reading about our lives together and how important it is for all rabbits to have a bunny companion wherever possible.

Being part of a human family also gives us greater quality of life.